J. OTTO SEIBOLD

LOST SLOTH

RING!!
RING!!

MᶜM
MᶜSWEENEY'S
MᶜMULLENS
www.mcsweeneys.net

Printed in China by Shanghai Offset · ISBN: 978-1-938073-35-9
First edition

The phone was ringing!

Sloth knew he'd better
hurry to answer it.

HURRY, SLOTH!

RING— CLICK!!

Sloth didn't hurry fast enough.

There was a voice talking into his answering machine. According to the voice, Sloth had won a prize, and the prize was a shopping spree!

Sloth was surprised and confused.

"What's a spree?" he thought.

CONGRATULATIONS
SLOTH! YOU WIN!
STARTS 3PM
YOU WIN!
STORE
SHOPPING SPREE!
SEE YOU THERE
TICK
HOTEL CARPET

Sloth had only three hours to claim his prize,
and the store was far away (for a sloth, at least).

He would need to hurry! So he jumped out
of his window, zipped down the clothesline...

...and flew over the backyard fence!

But oops—Sloth just missed the 532 bus.

If Sloth wanted his special prize,
he'd have to find another way to the store.

HURRY, SLOTH!

So Sloth decided to try something
he'd never tried before—a shortcut!

He entered the park and began moving,
slooooowly, through the trees.

HURRY, SLOTH!

The shortcut was working well until he
stopped to think about which way to go.

Sloth became sleepy.

Then sleepier…

**OH, NO!
WATCH OUT, SLOTH!**

...and then he fell out of the
tree and dropped right onto
an ice cream cart!

The ice cream man never saw Sloth.
(He had his eye on a bird.)

When Sloth awoke, he was the most lost he'd ever been. From a cliff high above town, he could see that he'd *never* make it to the store in time to claim his prize.

HURRY, SLOTH!
YOU'RE ALMOST THERE!
YOU CAN DO IT!

Then something
extraordinary happened!

In the next instant, Sloth
was flying way up in the
sky over everything!

**YAY, SLOTH!
LET'S GO, SLOTH!**

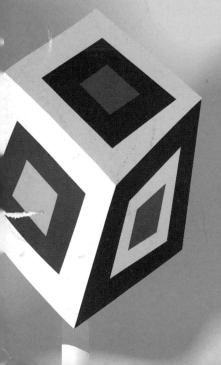

Sloth swooped into the front of the store—
through the automatic doors—and landed
on a shopping cart in the nick of time!

He was spree-ing!

**HOORAY, SLOTH!
WAY TO GO, SLOTH!**

Sloth was moving so fast that he shot straight through the store and crashed into a big pillow display!

Lots of different pillows fell into the cart, and Sloth landed on top of them.

He immediately passed out from all the excitement.

The store manager was impressed.

He carefully delivered Sloth back to his home without waking him up.

When Sloth arose the next morning,
he was surrounded by all the pillows
he'd won in the shopping spree!

He was so surprised and overjoyed
that he decided to celebrate with
a one-person pillow fight.

YAY, SLOTH! YOU WON!